GETRID

INTO THE PSYCHOPATH

Y AKHILESH

CHARCTERS : MORRIS,ASSAD,AURTHER,OLD MAN, CLOWN PIERCE AND SOME SIDE

CHARACTERS

FICTION BASED VIOLENCE,CRIME,THRILLER STORY

ONCE UPON A TIME IN SYRIA IN 2013 THERE USED TO LIVE A SINGLE PARENT 13YRS OLD CHILD

NAMED JASON MORRIS. HIS FATHER ASSAD WAS WORKING IN SYRIA MILITARY AS A SECRET A

AGENT,BUT FOR OTHERS HE WAS DOING IN A NORMAL SOFTWARE JOB .HIS MOTHER WAS

JULIEA QUEEN WHO WAS DEAD IN 2000 IT SELF. MORRIUS WAS GROWN FAR IN AN HOSTEL SO

HE DID NOT HAD A LOOK ON HIS EVERY ON MOTHER.

AFTER 2 YEARS

MORRIS DAD WAS DEAD AND HE WAS LIVING ALONE AND DOING A PARTIME JOB. ONE DAY HE

WAS GOING TO HIS JOB IN THE NIGHT CAUSE HE WAS 15 YEARS OLD AND HE NEEDS TO GO TO

LECTURE EVERY MORNING. ONE DAY MORRIS WENT TO HIS JOB AT NIGHT AND WHILE

COMING BACK HE SAW A OLD MAN WHO DRAGGED HIM TO A CORNER AND TOLD MORRIS

THAT "YOUR DAD IS A AGENT I KNOW HIM" BUT MORRIS IGNORES AND GOES HOME

MORRIS TOUCHED THE DOOR LOCK OF HIS FATHER`S ROOM AFTER 24MONTHS AND THEN

WITH IN SECONDS HIS DOOR BELL RINGS. MORRIS OPENS THE DOOR AND SEES POLICE.

A MAN TELLS "I AM AGENT AURTHER AND I AM HERE TO CHECK YOUR HOUSE CAUSE WE GOT

INFORMATION THAT YOU HAVE ILLEGAL WEAPONS WITH YOU" MORRIS CANT DO ANYTHING

EXCEPT WATCHING THEM RAID HIS HOUSE. POLICE BROKE HIS FATHER`S ROOM DOOR AND

THEY FOUND A PISTOL HIDDEN IN BOOKSHELF. POLICE ARRESTED MORRIS FOR AND TOOK

HIM TO STATION. LATER FEW DAYS MORRIS WAS TAKEN TO COURT AND WAS GIVEN PRISON

FOR 2 YEARS. AURTHER REQUESTED JUDGE TO GIVE MORE TIME FOR KNOWING WHOLE STORY

ABOUT HIM SO THE JUDGE GIVES 7 DAYS AND IN THIS 7 DAYS MORRIS WAS TORTURED A

LOT,BUT POLICE FOUND NOTHING SO MORRIS GOT A JAIL FOR 2YEARS

AFTER 2 YEARS

MORRIS WAS HOME AND WAS ANGRY THAT HE GOT JAIL FOR NO REASON,BUT HE CANT DO

NOTHING EXCEPT GOING TO THE OLD MAN. HE GOES TO THE CAME PLACEAT NIGHT IN HOPE

HE COULD FIND THAT OLD MAN AN DHE FINDS THAT OLD MAN HE ASKS WHY ARE THERE

WEAPONS IN MY HOME AND HOW YOU KNOW THAT. THERE ARE WEAPONS,BUT OLDMAN

TELLS IF YOU WANT TO FIND THE TRUTH THEN YOU NEED TO GO TO AURTER`S OFFICE AND

YOU SHOULD LOOK AT THE THIRD CASE , 2ND ROW AND 7TH FILE IN WHICH YOU MAY FIND

ANSWERS AND MORRIS GOES HOME FROM THERE. HE THINKS A LOT AND LOOKS AT HIS

FATHER`S ROOM. THEN HE ENTERED THE ROOM AND HE SAW THAT THERE ARE

2 PISTOLS,2DAGGARS AND 2 SWORDS WITH A BLACK DRESS HE WORE THE DRESS TAKES HIS

SWORDS AND HE GOES TO AURTHER`S OFFICE. WHEN HE WENT THERE. HE TOOK THE EXACT

FILE AND HE BEGINED TO GAIN TRUST ON THE OLD MAN WHEN HE TOOK A RANDOM PAGE

OUT A BULLET SHOT HIM ON HIS LEG AND HE WAS STUNNED CAUSE THE SHOOTER WAS

AURTHER AND HE USED A STUN GUN ON HIM.

THE FILE MAIN PAGE WAS IN THE FIRST AND IT CONTAINED OF INFORMATION ABOUT THE

PEOPLE IN THE OFFICE AND THEIR LIFE AND AT THE FIRST PAGE THERE WAS A ABOUT 4

AGENTS AND HOW THEY WORKED. THE FOUR AGENTS WERE ASSAD,REY,SPRITE, AND MURRAY

AND REY,SPRITE WERE MARRIED AND REY`S BROTHER WAS MURRAY. MURRAY HAD A

ADOPTED SON AND MURRAY WAS MISSING IN A PLANE CRASH AND THEY DECLARED HIM AS

DEAD AND THE ADOPTED SON WAS GIVEN TO REY AND SHE KEPT HIM IN HOSTEL FOR HIS

SAFTY, SPRITE AND REY WERE TAKEN DIVORCE AND REY WAS DEAD BY CANCER TEN LATER IN

2011 IN CIVIL WAR SPRITE WAS AGAINST GOVERNMENT AND ASSAD HAS NO CHOICE EXCEPT

BETRAYING AND KILLING HIM AND ASSAD TOOK THE CHILD. THE CHILD NAME WAS MORRS

HERE MORRIS LOOKED AT THE LAST PART WERE HE GOT TO KNOW THAT ASSAD KILLED HIS

DAD SPRITE.

MORRIS WOKE UP AND SAW HIMSELF IN A BED TIED UP TO THE BED. HE COULD NOT ESCAPE

AND THEN AURTHER ENTERED THE ROOM AND TOLD HIM THAT YOUR FATHER SPRITE IS A

BETRAYER AND WE DONT HAVE ANY CHOICE AND YOU SHOULD KNOW THAT I GOONA KILL IN

FEW HOURS AND HE TAKES THE FILE AND GOES OUT. HERE MORRIUS AS NOTHING TO DO SO

HE JUST STAYS CALM AND THINKS AND MORRIS WAS LUCKY THAT THE OLD MAN CAME IN

MINUTES AND HELPED HIM BREAK OUT.

OLD MAN AND MORRIS WENT TO THE OLD MAN`S HIDEOUT. MORRIS WAS ANGRY ON

ASSAD,BUT ASSAD WAS DEAD SO HE NEED TO KILL AURTHER CAUSE HE TOLD THAT HE WAS

ALSO A PART.MORRIS WAS GIVEN A RIFLE FROM THE OLDMAN SO THATIT COULD BE EASY

THEN HE WENT TO THE MALL WERE HE COULD FIND AURTHER ACCORDING TO THE OLD MAN.

HE FOUND AURTHER SO HE RUSHED INTO THE MALL BY KILLING THE GUARDS AND STARTED

FIRING RANDOMLY AT THE MALL.AURTHER WAS AGENT SO HE ESCAPED FROM THE MALL,BUT

HERE MORRIS DID NOT NOTICED AURTHER AND HE KILLED OVER 291 PEOPLE WITH HIS

RIFLE,PISTOLS,DAGGARS, AND SWORDS.

MORRIS WAS SORROUNDED BY POLICE AND HAS NOTHING TO DO EXCEPTING KILLING THEM

ONE BY ONE FROM STAYING IN THE MALL. MORRIS SHOOTED AT THE POLICE AND

WROTE *GETRID* ON THE WALL WITH BLOOD AND MORRIS ESCAPED FROM THERE. MORRIS WAS

AT OLD MAN'S HIDEOUT, THE OLD MAN YELLED AT HIM AND SAYED "YOU KILLED OVER 303

PEOPLE IN ONE DAY INCLUDING OLD MENS,OLD WOMENS AND SMALL CHILDREN ANDTHIS WAS

NOT ENOUGH THAT YOU WROTE GETRID WITH BLOOD OF ALL PEOPLE AND THREW THERE

BODIES IN FRONT OF THE WALL. PEOPLE ARE CALLING YOU GETRID AND THEY DECLARED YOU

AS A CRMINAL WITH 2MILLION DOLLORS BID ON YOU , BUT MORRIS WAS ANGRY AND HE

SHOOTED THE OLD MAN CAUSE HE WAS SHOUTING AT HIM.

MORRIS CAME TO KNOW THAT AURTHER IS IN A CINEMA HALL SO HE RUSHED TO THE CINEMA

HALL WERE HE FOUND SO MANY PEOPLE . ONCE AGAIN HE SHOUTED RANDOMLY AND HE WAS

KILLING EVERY ONE AGAIN AURTHER ESCAPED ,BUT THIS TIME MORRIS SAW HIM AFTER

KILLING ALL PEOPLE IN THE HALL HE RUSHED AT AURTHER WITH NO GUILT THAT HE KILLED

THIS MANY PEOPLE. GETRID CAUGHT AURTHER AND WAS ABOVE YO KILL HIM BUT THEN

AURTHER TOLD THAT ASSAD IS ALIVE AND HE IS IN VIETNAM IN HANOI. GET RID TOOK THE

EXACT LOCATION AND INFRONT OF ALL THE PEOPLE HE CUTTED AURTHER INTO HALF

MAKING THE MURDER A CRUIEL ONE.NOW GETRID FOUND A ILLEGAL WAY TO ENTER

VIETNAM AND WAS GOING TO KILL ASSAD.

NOW GETRID ENTERED VIETNAM AND WITH THE EXACT LOCATION AT NIGHT HE WENT TO

KILL ASSAD BUT THEN A BLACK SUITED MAN WITH A SWORD ARRIVED AND STOPPED

GETRID.THE MAN WAS A GOOD SWORDMAN AND HE AS A SWORD WHICH IS LITRALLY

CUTTING EVERY THING THEN WITH NO OPTION GETRID ESCAPED FROM THERE.

THE BLACK DRESS MAN WAS *CLOWN PIERCE*. ONCE UPON A TIME IN JAPAN THERE WERE 2

SWORDMEN VILLAGES AND ONE OF THE VILLAGE WAS ZANKOOPURAN AND CLOWN PIERCE`S

DAD WAS HEAS OF THAT VILLAGE AND CLOWN AS A SWORD MADE OF *H.C.U* [HARD

COMPRESSED URANIUM] WHICH IS STRONGEST METALAND WAS OWNED BY A MAN LI AND

LATER IT WAS GIVEN TO CLOWN PIERCE AND THAT SWORD NAME WAS *LI`S PIERCER* NO ONE

KNOWS HOW THEY GOT THAT SWORD BUT THE SWORD COSTS OVER 1.2TRILLION DOLLORS

CAUSE IT WAS THE ONLY PIECE.

LATER GETRID PLANTED 6 BOMBS. HE BLASTED THEM ALL AND KILLED OVER 1267 PEOPLE AND

WITH THE PAST KILLS IN SYRIA. GETRID KILLED OVER 1834. WHEN CLOWN SAW AT THE

PLACES GETRID PLANTED BOMBS HE SAW THAT HE PLANTED BOMBS AT HATES AVENUE,

AILLIATOWN , NORTORY MALL , OADIAN MALL , INIKE CINEMA HALL AND HE NOTICED THAT

HE REPRESENTED CITY HANOI WITH THE FIRST LETTERS

CLOWN RUSHED AT THE HANOI TO STOP GETRID FROM BLASTING THE BOMBS AND KILLING

ALL BUT T WHEN HE ENTERD GETRID ALREADY PLANTED THEM AND HE WANTED TO BLAST

THEM INFORNT OF CLOWN. THEY WERE IN MIDDLE OF THE CITY AND GETRID PLANTED AT

CORNERS SO THEY DONT HAVE DANGER. GETRID SHOOTED AT CLOWN PIERCE LEG AND MADE

HIM FALL.

GETRID KNEW THAT ASSAD IS AT HANOI AND THATS WHY HE DID THIS ALL. HE ENTERED TO

A HIGH BUILDING AND SAW ASSAD'S NAME IN THE LIST OF PEOPLE LIVING IN THE BUILDING.

HE RUSHED TO THE FLOOR AND SAW ASSAD. GETRID WAS ANGRY ON HIM THAT HE GETRID

TIED ASSAD TO CHAIR AND HE CUTTED ASSAD'S FINGERS OFF. GETRID ASKED WHY YOU

KILLED MY DAD THEN ASSAD SAID YOU ARE A PSYCHO YOU DONT KNOW THAT YOUR FATHER

IS NOT SPRITE HE IS MURRAY. ASSAD SHOWED THE EXACT FILE WHICH AURTHER AS AND

SHOWED THE PIC OF HIS FATHER MURRAY

GETRID WAS SHOCKED CAUSE MURRAY WAS ONLY THE OLD MAN HE KILLED AND THATS WHY

HE KNOW EVERY THING. GETRID ASKED ASSAD WHERE IS MY MOM THEN ASSAD TOLD THAT

YOU ARE ADOPTED BY MURRAY . THEN CLOWN PIERCE ENTERED THE FLOOR WITH BLEEDING

LEG, GETRID WAS SHOOTING ASSAD AND CLOWN PIERCE PUSHED GETRID FAR AWAY. BUT HE

WAS LATE AND ASSAD WAS DEAD AND WITH THE FORCE CLOWN PUSHED GETRID . GETRID

TACKLED THE WINDOW AND THE WINDOW BROKE AND GETRID WAS AT THE CORNER

HOLDING THE FLOOR AND IF HE FALLS HE WAS DEAD CAUSE HE WAS IN THE 32ND FLOOR.

CLOWN CAUGHT GETRID HAND AND SAID I WILL SAVE YOU BUT ING GUILT GETRID TOLD NO

AND HE PULLED CLOWN PIERCE`S HAND OFF FROM HIM AND COMMITED SUCIDE IN GUILT OF

KILLING HIS FATHER

NOTE : IF THERE ARE ANY SPELLING MISTAKES PLEASE FORGIVE ME AND IF THERE ARE ANY MISTAKES I WILL TRY TO IMPROVE MYSELF

Contents

Foreword

www.ingramcontent.com/pod-product-compliance
Lightning Source LLC
Chambersburg PA
CBHW022048150726
47990CB00004B/1652

* 9 7 9 8 8 8 7 7 2 6 9 8 4 *